SPONGEBOB ROUNDPANTS

adapted by Erica David
based on the teleplay by
Luke Brookshier, Nate Cash, and Steven Banks
illustrated by Dave Aikins

SCHOLASTIC INC.
New York Toronto London Auckland Sydney
Mexico City New Delhi Hong Kong Buenos Aires

W9-CII-444

Stephen Hillenburg

Based on the TV series *SpongeBob SquarePants*® created by Stephen Hillenburg as seen on Nickelodeon®

ISBN-13: 978-0-545-17417-6
ISBN-10: 0-545-17417-1

12 11 10 9 8 7 6 5 4 3 2 1   9 10 11 12 13 14/0

Printed in the U.S.A.

First Scholastic printing, September 2009

It was laundry day for SpongeBob. He gathered all of his dirty clothes and tossed them into a big pile.

"I love laundry day!" SpongeBob told his pet snail, Gary. "Everything gets cleaned!" And when SpongeBob said "everything," he meant *everything*—including the shell on Gary's back!

SpongeBob scooped up his clothes and dumped them into the washing machine. "Now I'll finish the day's chores," he said.

SpongeBob washed the dishes, vacuumed the floor, and dusted the furniture.

Then he put his clothes in the dryer, just as Patrick called on the phone.

"Hi, SpongeBob. You wanna hear how long I can make this sound?" asked Patrick. Before SpongeBob could reply, Patrick began to yodel loudly into the phone.

An hour later Patrick was still yodeling. SpongeBob tried to interrupt him, but it was no use. Once Patrick started yodeling, there was no stopping him.

SpongeBob looked at the clock. His clothes were probably dry by now. "Gary, go check the laundry," he whispered.

Gary inched his way into the laundry room. He opened the dryer and took out his shell. It was dry and still warm. Gary was so happy to have his shell back that he forgot all about SpongeBob's clothes.

When SpongeBob finally got off the phone, he hurried to check on the laundry. He was shocked to see that his clothes were still in the dryer. He stopped the machine and took out his pants—only to find that they had shrunk!

"Oh, no! I'm going to need new pants," he said sadly.

Later that day SpongeBob went to shop for pants. But when he walked into his favorite store, Nautical Knickers, he got some bad news.

"I'm sorry, sir," the store clerk said. "We're out of square pants. It looks like we won't be getting another shipment for months. But perhaps you'll find another style to meet your needs."

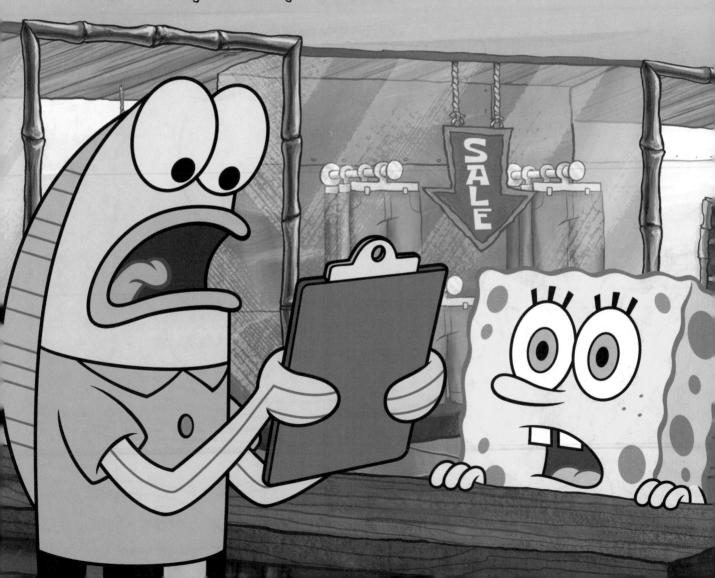

SpongeBob tried on all kinds of pants, but he couldn't find anything that he liked. The pants were either too long . . .

too wide . . .

or just plain too weird.

SpongeBob was about to give up when he found a pair of pants that were almost too good to be true. He tried them on—and they were a perfect fit!

"These round pants hug my body better than my own mother!" he exclaimed.

A short while later SpongeBob left the store wearing his new pants. On his way home he saw Patrick.

"Hey, Patrick," SpongeBob called out. "Notice anything different?"

"Sorry, do I know you?" Patrick asked, confused.

"Patrick, I'm SpongeBob!" SpongeBob said.

Patrick looked at a drawing of SpongeBob on his hand. "No, you're not! SpongeBob wears *square* pants. Now leave me alone, you mysterious stranger!" Patrick said, before walking away in a huff.

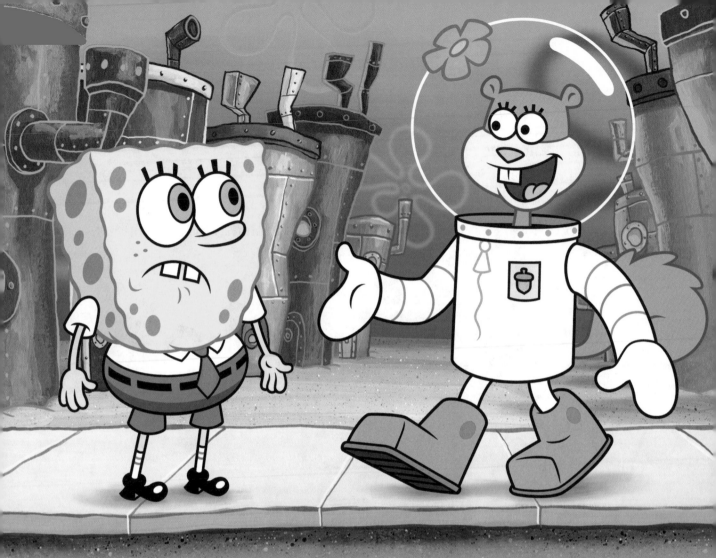

SpongeBob couldn't believe it. "It's just new pants," he said. "It's not like my friends won't recognize me."

At that moment Sandy walked by. "Howdy, stranger," she said to SpongeBob. "I don't recognize you in those newfangled dungarees."

SpongeBob was shocked—Sandy didn't recognize him either! The pants really made him look like a different person!

SpongeBob kept walking. He was almost home when he spotted Squidward. Squidward will recognize me, he thought.

"Hi, Squidward!" SpongeBob said brightly.

"Do I know you?" Squidward asked, annoyed. He was pretending not to recognize SpongeBob so he wouldn't have to talk to him. But SpongeBob believed that Squidward really didn't know who he was.

SpongeBob walked away feeling a little sad. I guess I'm not SpongeBob SquarePants anymore, he thought. I'll have to start all over again.

SpongeBob wandered around for a while, not sure what to do. Hours later he spotted the Krusty Krab, which cheered him up immediately.

"I'm ready! I'm ready! I'm ready!" SpongeBob yelled happily as he headed toward the restaurant.

When SpongeBob arrived at the Krusty Krab, he marched straight to the cashier's counter.

"Hello, Mr. Cashier!" SpongeBob said. "My name is SpongeBob Square . . . I mean, SpongeBob RoundPants, and I'd like to apply for a position at this fine eating establishment."

Squidward nearly fell over. His plan to pretend not to know SpongeBob hadn't worked! SpongeBob was back to pester him!

Squidward had no choice but to play along. He handed SpongeBob a job application.

As SpongeBob filled it out, Mr. Krabs walked in. "What is going on here?" he asked.

"I'm filling out a job application," SpongeBob explained.

"Get to work!" ordered Mr. Krabs.

"You mean I got the job? Hooray!" exclaimed SpongeBob.

SpongeBob couldn't wait to
start his job. He put on his Krusty
Krab hat and turned to Squidward.
"You've worked here a long time.
How about showing this rookie
the ropes?"

"I'd *love* to," Squidward said, not meaning it at all. He led SpongeBob
around the restaurant, showing him what to do. In no time SpongeBob
learned how Squidward did his job—and picked up all of his bad habits.

The next day SpongeBob did his job just the way Squidward had shown him. He was rude to the customers, he burned the Krabby Patties, and he kept going to the bathroom. Squidward was proud of him.

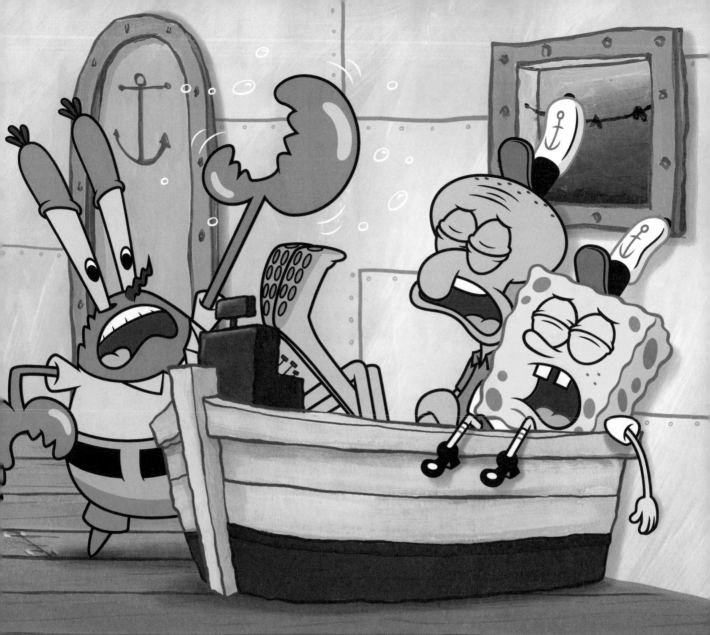

When Mr. Krabs walked into the restaurant, he was shocked to see a long line of angry customers—and both SpongeBob and Squidward asleep at the register.

"What are you two doing?" Mr. Krabs yelled. "I'm used to Squidward sleeping on the job, but I expect more from you, Mr. SquarePants!"

"I am not SpongeBob SquarePants, Mr. Krabs," SpongeBob replied.

"What are you talking about?" Mr. Krabs asked angrily.

"Do these pants look square to you? They're round. I can't be
SpongeBob SquarePants with round pants," explained SpongeBob.
"Well, why don't you just take off the pants?" suggested Mr. Krabs.
"That's a great idea!" SpongeBob said.

Moments later SpongeBob came out of the kitchen in his underpants.

"Order up, Squidward!" he cried, happy to be SpongeBob SquarePants again, and to be serving up delicious, well-cooked Krabby Patties with a smile.

Just then Sandy walked into the Krusty Krab and noticed SpongeBob right away. "Well, well, if it isn't SpongeBob *Under*Pants," she said.

SpongeBob screamed. It had been bad enough being SpongeBob RoundPants. Now he'd have to start all over as SpongeBob *Under*Pants!